EDGE BOOKS

DINOSAUR WARS

DEINONYCHUS

★★★★★★★★★★★

VS.

STYRACOSAURUS

★★★★★★★★★★★

WHEN CLAWS AND SPIKES COLLIDE

by Michael O'Hearn

Consultant:
Mathew J. Wedel, PhD
Paleontologist and Assistant Professor
Western University of Health Sciences
Pomona, California

CAPSTONE PRESS
a capstone imprint

Edge Books are published by Capstone Press,
1710 Roe Crest Drive, North Mankato, Minnesota 56003.
www.capstonepub.com

 Books published by Capstone Press are manufactured with paper
containing at least 10 percent post-consumer waste.

Library of Congress Cataloging-in-Publication Data
O'Hearn, Michael, 1972–
    Deinonychus vs. Styracosaurus : when claws and spikes collide / by Michael O'Hearn.
    p. cm.—(Edge books. Dinosaur wars)
    Summary: "Describes the features of Deinonychus and Styracosaurus, and how they
may have battled each other in prehistoric times"—Provided by publisher.
    Includes bibliographical references and index.
    ISBN 978-1-4296-4757-1 (library binding)
    1. Deinonychus—Juvenile literature. 2. Styracosaurus—Juvenile literature.
I. Title. II. Series.
QE862.S3.O343 2011
567.912—dc22   2010000986

Editorial Credits
Aaron Sautter and Jenny Marks, editors; Kyle Grenz, designer;
    Wanda Winch, media researcher; Nathan Gassman, art director;
    Laura Manthe, production specialist

Illustrations
Jon Hughes: 9, 12, 14, 19 (top)
Philip Renne: 5, 20–29

Photo Credits
Alamy/amberstock, 11; Friedrich Saurer, 13; McPhoto/vario images, 8
Capstone/James Field, 4, 10; Steve Weston, 17
Raul Lunia, cover (all), 6 (all) 16, 18 (bottom), 19 (bottom)
Shutterstock/Leigh Prather, stylized backgrounds; Ralf Juergen Kraft,
    15, 19 (middle); Steve Cukrov, 18 (top); Valery Potapova,
    parchment backgrounds

TABLE OF CONTENTS

WELCOME TO DINOSAUR WARS!

Dinosaurs were brutal creatures. They fought each other and ate each other. Usually it was meat-eater versus plant-eater or big versus small. But in Dinosaur Wars, it's a free-for-all. Plant-eaters attack plant-eaters. Giants fight giants. And small dinosaurs gang up on huge opponents. In Dinosaur Wars, any dinosaur battle is possible!

In this dinosaur war, Deinonychus goes on the hunt for Styracosaurus. You'll learn about Deinonychus' weapons and fighting style. You'll also discover that Styracosaurus has weapons of his own, and he's not afraid to use them. Then you'll see these fierce beasts battle head-to-head—and you'll get to watch from a front row seat!

Deinonychus (dye-NON-ik-uhs)
Styracosaurus (stih-RAK-uh-sore-uhs)

THE COMBATANTS

DEINONYCHUS VS. STYRACOSAURUS

Deinonychus and Styracosaurus never fought. These dinosaurs lived at least 30 million years apart from each other. Styracosaurus walked the earth about 77 million years ago until becoming **extinct** 70 million years ago. Deinonychus lived on Earth from about 100 to 110 million years ago.

However, if they had lived at the same time, they may have bumped into each other. **Fossils** of Deinonychus were found in northern Wyoming. Styracosaurus fossils were discovered in Alberta, Canada. Bones of both dinosaurs have also been found in Montana.

Scientists can tell the age of a fossil by looking at how many layers of rock it was buried under.

FIERCE FACT
FOSSIL AGE

extinct—no longer living anywhere in the world
fossil—the remains of an animal preserved as rock

SIZE

Styracosaurus was about the size of a large SUV. From nose to tail, he was about 18 feet (5.5 meters) long. He weighed as much as 3 tons (2.7 metric tons). In the dinosaur world, he wasn't especially large. His cousin Triceratops weighed as much as 10 tons (9 metric tons). But compared to Deinonychus, Styracosaurus was a giant.

Deinonychus stood about 5 feet (1.5 m) tall. From nose to tail, he was 10 feet (3 m) long. He weighed about 150 pounds (68 kilograms). To say these dinosaurs were a mismatch in size would be an understatement. Styracosaurus definitely held a size advantage.

SPEED AND AGILITY

Deinonychus was built for running. His legs were long and slender, and he had a lightweight frame. His stiff tail stuck straight out to give him balance and help him make quick, sharp turns. His long legs were also perfect for leaping onto the backs of large **prey**.

prey—an animal that is hunted by another animal

10

Before the discovery of Deinonychus, most scientists thought dinosaurs were slow and unintelligent.

FIERCE
FACT
DISCOVERY

Styracosaurus stood low to the ground, where he found most of his food. His weight rode directly above his sturdy legs. Scientists think his top speed was about 20 miles (32 kilometers) per hour. But he likely only ran in short, powerful charges. His body was not built to run fast for very long. Deinonychus would definitely have the speed advantage in a fight.

DEFENSES

Deinonychus was a fierce **predator**. This dino's ferocious nature would have kept him out of most danger. Deinonychus' speed also served as a defense. Larger predators had to catch Deinonychus before they could eat him. This was not an easy task.

predator—an animal that hunts and eats other animals

The name Styracosaurus
means "spiked lizard."

Styracosaurus had a spiky shield built into his head. Each edge of his frill had several sharp spikes. The frill wasn't solid, so it probably couldn't deflect a direct attack. But it did provide some protection for his neck. The sharp spikes would make it hard for a predator to get too close.

Styracosaurus may have also traveled in herds for protection. A predator would have to think twice before attacking a large group of these spiky plant-eaters.

WEAPONS

Deinonychus
Deadly teeth and claws
★ ★ ★ ★

★ ★ ★
Styracosaurus
Sharp horn and spikes

Deinonychus attacked prey with several knifelike weapons. His **serrated** teeth could slice through flesh. He could hold his prey close with three clawed fingers on each hand. Each foot had a sharp, hooked toe claw that could rip into an enemy. This deadly combination made it tough for enemies to get anywhere near Deinonychus without suffering serious injuries.

serrated—having a jagged edge

Styracosaurus was armed and dangerous too. His main weapon was a sharp 2-foot (0.6-m) nose horn. His sharp frill spikes protected Styracosaurus from any enemy that dared to come too close. Styracosaurus also had a sharp beak and powerful jaws. His painful bite could definitely do some damage.

The horns and spikes of some dinosaurs, such as Styracosaurus, were covered with a hard substance called keratin. Human hair and fingernails are also made from keratin.

FIERCE FACT

KERATIN

ATTACK STYLE

As a **herbivore**, Styracosaurus usually didn't like to pick fights. But if he felt threatened, he was equipped to protect himself. With enough open ground, Styracosaurus could charge and pierce an opponent with his deadly nose horn. He could also jab the enemy with his sharp frill spikes. If he found an opening, he could bite anything within reach of his sharp beak.

herbivore—an animal that eats only plants

Over time, many meat-eating dinosaurs grew larger to kill big plant-eaters. But Deinonychus, like other raptor dinosaurs, stayed small and fast.

FIERCE FACT

STAYING SMALL

Deinonychus probably hunted in packs to increase his chances of getting food. But even by himself, he was a fierce and savage **carnivore**. He would leap onto his target and grab hold with his strong hand claws. Then he slashed at his victim's throat and belly with his deadly toe claws. In spite of his smaller size, Deinonychus could take down prey larger than himself.

carnivore—an animal that eats only meat

17

GET READY TO RUMBLE!

This dinosaur battle is sure to be downright brutal. In one corner is the ferocious hunter—Deinonychus! He'll start a fight before his victim knows what's happening. In the other corner is the peaceful plant-eater—Styracosaurus! He just wants to be left alone, but he's deadly when he gets angry. It's anyone's guess which beast will be left standing.

You've got a front row seat. So grab your favorite snack and drink, turn the page, and get ready to enjoy the battle!

DEINONYCHUS

SIZE ★ ★ ★ ★ ★

SPEED AND AGILITY ★ ★ ★ ★ ★ ★ ★ ★

DEFENSES ★ ★ ★

WEAPONS ★ ★ ★ ★ ★ ★

ATTACK STYLE ★ ★ ★ ★ ★ ★ ★

STYRACOSAURUS

ONE LAST THING...

This battle is fake. It's made-up, just like your favorite comic book. In real life, these dinosaurs never met. Nobody knows how they would have battled, or which beast would have won. Yet this matchup is sure to be a bloody and deadly smackdown!

PAIN

A herd of Styracosaurus stomps past some scattered trees. Small clouds of dust puff up where their feet pound the earth. The females and their young are gathered in the middle of the group. The large males hover near the edge. Their tall frill spikes surround the herd like a fence.

One young Styracosaurus stops beside a tree to munch a clump of ferns. The herd rumbles past him as he ducks his head and chews. A large male nudges the youngster with his snout as he passes.

The young straggler takes one last bite and scurries after his herd. Suddenly, a wild screech erupts behind him. He turns to see a blur of dust, claws, and snapping teeth behind him. A pack of Deinonychus is on the hunt!

A baby Styracosaurus had only a small frill when it hatched. Babies did not have nose horns or frill spikes. Their spiky defenses didn't grow until they got older.

FIERCE FACT

BABY DEFENSES

FIERCE FACT

PACK HUNTERS

Deinonychus fossil sites suggest that the dinosaurs hunted in packs. Deinonychus fossils are sometimes found surrounding large plant-eating dinosaurs called Tenontosaurus.

The young Styracosaurus grunts and bolts toward his herd. A large male charges out to meet him. He races to reach the youngster before the pack of hunters gets there. But the meat-eaters are too fast.

Three of the attackers pounce on the young Styracosaurus. One bites at his neck. Another leaps onto the youngster's back. A third grabs on and starts slashing at his victim's belly with his deadly toe claws. The young Styracosaurus slumps forward and crumples to the ground. The three attackers feast on their kill.

The remaining Deinonychus speed toward the herd. One attacker races to the charging adult Styracosaurus. The heavy beast lowers his nose horn before colliding with the meat-eater. The Deinonychus screeches as the deadly spike slices through him. The Styracosaurus jerks his head and flings his enemy's body to the ground.

The last two Deinonychus continue scrambling toward the Styracosaurus herd. Suddenly, a shriek is heard from the edge of the woods. Two more Deinonychus burst out from the trees to join the frantic race to their prey.

The herd doesn't panic. Instead, the big beasts slow down. The large males turn to face their screeching enemies. The males stand shoulder-to-shoulder and frill-to-frill. Their nose horns point toward the oncoming predators. The large beasts growl a warning to keep away.

The four Deinonychus stop and stare at the line of spikes before them. It's a scary sight, even for the fierce hunters.

Finally, one Deinonychus bolts toward the herd. The males lower their spiked heads and hold their ground.

The hunter races straight at them. At the last instant, he leaps. He sails over the horns and lands among the herd. He latches onto an adult female Styracosaurus. He digs his front claws into her flesh and slashes at her with his toe claws.

The plant-eaters panic. Two frightened youngsters dash away from the herd. A large male strikes the invading Deinonychus with his horn. He jerks his nose upward again and again, stabbing the predator. Finally the Deinonychus goes limp and slides off the bloodied body of the female.

The three remaining hunters spot the two fleeing Styracosaurus. Eager for a meal, the hunters rush toward the fleeing prey. One young Styracosaurus uses his growing nose horn to stab and jab the attackers. He catches one of the hunters and sends him tumbling. Then he dashes toward the safety of his herd.

Behind him, the remaining youngster struggles to break free. The predators rip into him with their teeth and claws. A pair of large male Styracosaurus charge out to help, but they're too late. The small, bloodied Styracosaurus squeals and crashes to the ground.

The adults stop. They can only watch as the hunters bury their sharp teeth into the fallen victim. The adults return to the herd, which starts moving again. The large animals moan lowly as they stomp across the dusty earth. Behind them, a Deinonychus shrieks triumphantly over its hard-earned meal.

Deinonychus was named after its deadliest weapon. "Deinonychus" means terrible claw.

FIERCE FACT

NAME

GLOSSARY

carnivore (KAHR-nuh-vohr)—an animal that eats only meat

extinct (ik-STINGKT)—no longer living; an extinct animal is one whose kind has died out completely

fossil (FAH-suhl)—the remains or traces of plants and animals that are preserved as rock

herbivore (HUR-buh-vor)—an animal that eats only plants

predator (PRED-uh-tur)—an animal that hunts other animals for food

prey (PRAY)—an animal hunted by another animal for food

serrated (SER-ay-tid)—having a jagged edge that helps with cutting, such as a saw blade

READ MORE

Long, John A. *Dinosaurs*. New York: Simon & Schuster Books for Young Readers, 2007.

Mash, Robert. *Extreme Dinosaurs*. New York: Atheneum, 2007.

Matthews, Rupert. *Dinosaur Combat: Unearth the Secrets Behind Dinosaur Fossils*. Dinosaur Dig. Laguna Hills, Calif.: QEB Publishing, 2008.

INTERNET SITES

FactHound offers a safe, fun way to find Internet sites related to this book. All of the sites on FactHound have been researched by our staff.

Here's all you do:

Visit *www.facthound.com*

Type in this code: 9781429647571

INDEX